Dire Consequences

Dire Consequences:

The Formula
No Sign Posted
All In Due Time

Jaci Risser

Strategic Book Publishing
Durham, Connecticut

Strategic Book Publishing
An imprint of Strategic Book Group
P. O. Box 333
Durham, CT 06422
http://www.StrategicBookGroup.com

ISBN: 978-1-60911-111-3

Book Design: Julius Kiskis

Printed in the United States of America
18 17 16 15 14 13 12 11 10   1 2 3 4 5

Dedication

To my niece, Beci.

THE FORMULA

ONE

The rain had been a steady downpour since Sara first woke. Her son, Tyler, would be getting up soon for school. Or at least Sara would soon be trying to get him up in time for school. In the meantime, Sara would have some quiet time to herself to drink her coffee and review her day's agenda.

Allan, Sara's husband, was out of town for the week at his company's sales convention. He called last night to say he arrived safely and missed them. Sara knew it was true, but it was also true that Allan would be too busy to think about them for the next five days. As the national sales manager, he was responsible for this entire program and spent the greater part of the last two months preparing for it. The company sales' projections for the next year were aggressive and this past year had been a disappointment, so everyone had their work cut out for them.

Sara turned to look at the family's cat who was perched

attentively near her on the sofa. As Sara reached out her hand, the cat moved closer and rubbed her head against the welcome hand. Chelsea was a kind natured cat who responded warmly to her family and even to close friends. Sara chirped a few words of love to her which prompted some serious purring.

Next was the trip into the kitchen for Chelsea's breakfast and Sara's second cup of coffee. With Chelsea enjoying her meal and Sara relishing her final sips of coffee, the morning was off to it's usual, good start. This was precious time to Sara because, although she worked from home on a part-time basis, her days were very full. This time in the morning allowed her to envision what she needed to accomplish from both a work standpoint and home and family responsibilities.

Today would be a fun day for Sara because she would be shooting birds and wildlife, shooting from a camera that is. As a freelance photographer, Sara enjoyed the first day of her shoots. Upon receiving an assignment, she would plan what she wanted to photograph and then proceed to take many, many pictures that would later be edited. The editing process included deleting a lot of pictures and editing many others by zooming into an image or blurring a background to emphasize another part of the photo. Editing was also fun for Sara, but a more critical eye was needed. The editing process also taught Sara more about how to take better pictures the next time around.

Today's assignment was to shoot candid shots around her neighborhood of birds, squirrels, rabbits, etc. in their daily routines. The backdrop would be the neighboring homes and would be used in a brochure to sell life and health insurance. After Sara sorted through her pictures and decided on ten to fifteen of her best shots to submit to the client, they would choose one or two of them for their ad campaign.

Sara needed to get on with the morning routine when she heard a loud bang coming from next door. Mr. Robertson lived there and kept very much to himself. It appeared he lived alone and had few, if any, visitors. Sara had tried to make small talk with him from time to time, but he cut her off and went into his home. His home was the least attractive home on the block. The neighborhood children labeled his house the "spooky house". Tyler would sometimes brag that he lived next door to the spooky house and that it didn't scare him.

The truth be told, Tyler went out of his way to avoid Mr. Robertson and tried not to look at the dark, unkempt yard that stared at him from his bedroom window. His parents knew this and when he said he liked his blinds closed all the time, they gave no argument. The family moved into this house two years ago when Allan was transferred there. Soon afterward, Mr. Robertson moved into the house next door. It didn't take long for things to deteriorate. Within six months, the yard was filled with weeds and overgrown grass. No lights were seen coming from either inside the house or outside, with the exception of one dim light radiating from a small basement window, night after night.

Rumors began amongst both the children and the adults

in the neighborhood. Perhaps Mr. Robertson was an insomniac, guessed the adults. The children were certain he kept something or someone in the basement and spent all his time there. On a rare occasion, Mr. Robertson could be seen scurrying back and forth from the house to his garage. He carried small paper bags that presumably held food, but made little conversation with neighbors. A nod of his head or grunt was his usual response to a persistent neighbor.

Sara went to her sun porch to investigate the loud noise she heard. The rain dwindled down to a trickle. She didn't see anything out of the ordinary at Mr. Robertson's house. Looking at the clock, Sara realized it was time for Tyler to get up and ready for school.

After a few stern warnings, he was up, dressed and eating breakfast when he asked his mom about the loud noise. Surprised he had heard it, Sara told him she didn't know but it was probably nothing. Grabbing his lunch, Tyler headed out to the corner to wait for the bus. He always went through the front door, but today he went out the sliding glass door from the sun porch to get a view of Mr. Robertson's yard. Nothing different today, so he proceeded around his house to the front. As he walked he sensed someone there and looked up. Mr. Robertson was staring at him from less than ten feet away. Tyler jumped and dropped his backpack. Silently Mr. Robertson nodded, and then his mouth opened to a big toothy grin that revealed a shiny gold tooth. This was not the first time Mr. Robertson had done this exact thing. On several occasions, he would look at Tyler and smile with that gold tooth, but only when no one else was around. Silently, Tyler grabbed his backpack and ran.

Two

On the bus Tyler told his best friend, Jake, about seeing Mr. Robertson that morning. The boys decided they should try to snoop around his property to find out why he was so strange and quiet. They were sure they would find someone being kept in the basement and it seemed like a great adventure awaited them once they finished their day of school and soccer practice.

Meantime, Sara cleaned her camera and lenses. She knew the park nearby would be a good spot because several houses backed up to it. On her way out the door, she heard that loud bang again. This time she thought, "I'm going over to Mr. Robertson's and find out if everything is okay."

Knocking on Mr. Robertson's front door, Sara glanced around and noticed several squirrels and rabbits going about their day's business in the overgrown grass and bushes. The doorbell was clearly not working, so Sara knocked again harder. When there was still no answer,

Sara decided to go to the back door and knock because Mr. Robertson usually went in and out of that door. It was an interesting walk to the back door because the wildlife was especially active that day. The sun was shining through the trees and with Sara's eye for a good picture, she couldn't help but contemplate getting her camera out and shooting a few pictures.

Still, the reason for her being there was to be sure her neighbor was okay. Sara knocked vigorously on the back door. After several attempts and no response, Sara thought it wouldn't hurt if she stayed around for a few more minutes and took some pictures while she was waiting. As she moved about the yard to get in position for the shots, Sara thought she saw something flickering in the basement. She went over to the window and looked in but it was covered with some kind of paper. Not able to see anything in the window, Sara worked on getting her shots of the squirrels and rabbits. She was moving around the yard, shooting the animals as they gathered nuts and buried them, when again she saw the flicker coming from the basement. This time she was certain of it and began to feel something was not right.

She was putting her cameras into her bag with her head down when a low deep voice came up behind her. "What are you doing?" asked Mr. Robertson.

Startled, Sara said, "I heard a loud noise here this morning a couple times and came over to check on you."

"Ah ha, so you take pictures of people's property when you

come to check on them?" was Mr. Robertson's retort.

Sara responded, "I am a photographer and only took pictures of the wildlife in your yard. I was waiting a bit to see if you would be coming home." Sara felt that even with good intentions, Mr. Robertson was not going to see her point.

Scowling, Mr. Robertson said, "Everything is fine here. You must be mistaken."

Sara knew that she would not be able to get him to believe she was trying to help, so she simply said, "I hope everything is all right, Mr. Robertson. I'll be on my way now."

Sara was concerned because she knew what she heard and also knew that her neighbor did not want help. Refocusing on her business for that day, Sara went about taking pictures throughout the neighborhood and would develop them tonight after dinner.

Tyler and Jake were eager to get home after soccer practice because they still had it in their minds that it was up to them to find out what Mr. Robertson was hiding.

With her husband out of town and Tyler playing outside, Sara decided to work on editing the shots that she took that day. Her computer, along with Photoshop software, was all she used these days to edit her photographs. She needed every spare minute to get through all the pictures and edit the best ones so that she could turn in the final pictures to the insurance company in two days.

As Sara reviewed and edited her pictures, the boys plotted their mission to uncover the mystery at Mr. Robertson's house. Jake would ring the front door bell and Tyler would sneak around the back to find a way to look into the house or at least get a good view of that basement window. The reason for Jake's visit would be to ask Mr. Robertson if he would buy a magazine subscription for their soccer fundraiser. If, or rather when, Mr. Robertson refused, Jake would start crying and tell him he hasn't sold but three and they were all to family members. The boys did not expect sympathy from their strange neighbor; they were simply buying time.

It was starting to get dark and that added to the boys' excitement. They had no idea how far their plan would go and the darkness made it even more uncertain. Jake walked up the path to Mr. Robertson's house, as Tyler stood poised at the back gate to quickly enter and perform his part of the mission.

Bolding ringing the doorbell, Jake prepared his best salesman face of bright anticipation. After the third time he rang the bell, Jake took a deep breath and knocked hard on the door since the bell was obviously not working. Soon shuffling footsteps could be heard from within the house. Without so much as turning on the porch light, Mr. Robertson's bellowed out, "Go away. I don't want anything!"

Jake was caught off guard, but recovered quickly, saying, "Mr. Robertson, may I speak with you for just a second?"

Jerking open the door just enough to poke his head out,

Mr. Robertson glared at him and asked, "What is it, boy?"

Speaking louder than normal for Tyler's benefit, Jake said, "Sir, would you please consider buying a magazine subscription for our fundraiser?" Without a word, Mr. Robertson moved to slam the door in Jake's face, but Jake was not going to be defeated so quickly. "Sir, our fundraiser helps children with cancer. Won't you please take a look at the list of magazines? There's got to be one that interests you."

With a sneer on his face, Mr. Robertson shouted, "Raising money to fight cancer is a ridiculous waste of time. Get off my property before I call the police." With the door slammed in his face, Jake took stock of his efforts and decided that he had given Tyler at least two minutes to poke around the backyard. Leaving Mr. Robertson's house and heading around back to Tyler's house, Jake looked up to see Tyler running at him. "I saw him! There's someone in that basement and he looks just like Mr. Robertson, only older. He's keeping his father in the basement!"

Jake looked at Tyler and in his vast life experience said, "That's not so weird. A lot of people have their parents living in the basement. They set up their own apartment down there."

"There's nothing set up down there. It's a dark, creepy basement and the old man is lying on a cot!" exclaimed Tyler. Looking at Jake to emphasize his point, he said slowly, "He looks dead."

"Okay, now that part is weird," admitted Jake.

"You darn right, it's weird," responded Tyler. "I only got a quick look, but something is going on down there that is not normal. There's laboratory stuff all around and microscopes. He probably killed him and is trying to find a way to get rid of the body."

"I need to get home for dinner. Call me later," said Jake as he walked in the direction of his house.

"Don't talk about this to anyone! Mr. Robertson could be a murderer, but we need more information before we can go to the police," said Tyler.

Walking into his house, Tyler called out to his mom. She answered with, "I'm on the phone with your dad. Just a minute." Even his mom sounded strange. Usually she sounded relaxed talking to his dad or was laughing about something. Tonight she was speaking in a hushed tone and sounded irritated at Tyler.

Walking by his parents' bedroom, Tyler caught part of the conversation that stopped him in his tracks. "I know there's something going on in that basement, Allan. I have it on film."

Tyler waited for his mom at the kitchen table. She walked in looking disheveled and said, "Did you wash up for dinner, honey?"

"Yep. What were you talking to dad about?"

"Oh, just some work that I'm doing and needed his opinion."

"I heard you say something about the basement. Were you talking about Mr. Robertson's basement?" asked Tyler.

Surprised, Sara answered carefully, "Now, what makes you think that? I was talking about a leak in our basement. It's near my old dark room." Sara certainly did not want her son to feel scared about their next-door neighbor. She would sort this out with Allan when he got home in a few days.

"Okay, Mom. Don't tell me. But I know what you said." They ate their meal with little conversation and afterward Tyler went to his room to do homework.

The second he finished his homework, he went to get the cordless phone in the kitchen to call Jake. His mom was on the phone again. This time, she was in her bedroom with the door closed and Tyler could not hear what she was saying. "Mom, I need to use the phone," Tyler called out to her.

"Okay, I need a couple more minutes and then you can use it," she answered. Sara had called her best friend, Joanne, and told her what she had found. While she was shooting pictures in Mr. Robertson's yard, she had inadvertently gotten his basement window in several of the shots. There was a bright light coming from the window that the pictures captured. Sara then enlarged the photos and in one picture in particular, saw that the light in the basement was very bright, like in a laboratory. Now why would Mr. Robertson, who was very much up in age, have a need for special lighting in his basement? And what was it that caused that loud noise twice yesterday that Mr. Robertson refused to acknowledge? Joanne had agreed that there were some unusual things occurring at his house, but pointed out that people have a right to privacy as long as they don't break the law. Sara realized that she was right, but in her gut she felt something was definitely not right.

Tyler called Jake as planned, but Jake's mom said he was already asleep. Tyler wasn't sure he believed her because Jake was not one to sleep when an exciting plot was developing in the neighborhood. He would have to wait to talk to Jake until the morning, but sleep was not going to come easily that night for him.

As Tyler lay awake in his bed, he peered out his blinds into Mr. Robertson's yard. Tyler nearly jumped out of bed when he saw that light glowing from the basement. He ran downstairs and into his backyard before thinking what he would do when he got there. He was certain he heard someone moving around in the yard next door. Thankful for the darkness, Tyler flattened himself against the side of his house and listened intently. It sounded like someone was dragging something.

As the minutes ticked on, the sound decreased. Tyler was not able to look over into the yard for fear of being discovered. Feeling that whatever was going on was now done and therefore it would be safe to move, Tyler slowly inched himself off the brick of his house and turned to go inside. Out of the corner of his eye, he saw Mr. Robertson's face in the moonlight. Though willing himself not to turn and look directly at him, his head moved with a will of its own. Eye to eye, Tyler faced Mr. Robertson for a split second. Then Tyler turned and ran into his house. What Tyler didn't see was a body lying in the weeds next to Mr. Robertson.

With sweat pouring down his face, he nearly collided with his mother on his way up the stairs. "Tyler, what is going on?" she asked.

"N-Nothing. I needed a drink of water," Tyler lied. He didn't want to lie, but telling his mother he had been spying on Mr. Robertson earlier and saw a man in his basement and just now had seen Mr. Robertson in the dark did not seem like a good idea.

"Please get into bed. It's late. Are you sure you're okay?" asked his mother.

"Yeah, I'm okay. Good night, Mom," answered Tyler. In his bed with his door locked, he went over in his head the peculiar activities he witnessed today. None of it made sense and eventually sleep overtook him.

Sara kept the pictures showing the strange light coming from the basement on her bed and pondered them. She eventually told herself it was a special light used to help houseplants grow and with that assumption, she too fell asleep.

However, someone nearby was not sleeping that night. Mr. Robertson had work to do and not a lot of time. That boy knocking on his door and then later walking home alone was fortuitous and he would need to work through the night to make the final adjustment to his formula. His formula would change the world. It was worth everything and all the sacrifices that had to be made. Mr. James Robertson's Formula would make him immortal. His formula made living forever possible through acquiring new DNA. Once he was able to mass produce it, he would sell it to wealthy individuals who were willing to pay anything for eternal youth.

THREE

The next morning dawned bright and sunny. The April showers had indeed brought May flowers. Grass was greening up everywhere and spring flowers were beginning to sprinkle the landscape. Sara called to Tyler, "Time to get up, honey. Please don't make me late. I have a meeting this morning and need to leave in thirty minutes."

Tyler rolled over and for a second forgot everything on his mind from yesterday. Then it all came back to him and he jolted up. He was downstairs eating his breakfast in record time when his mother commented, "Thanks for getting right up. I have some paperwork here for you to bring to school. Is Jake still sleeping over tonight?"

It was Friday and once a month the boys alternated houses for a sleepover. "Yeah, as far as I know he is," answered Tyler.

Sara and her son parted ways, with Sara giving Tyler a

cell phone today. "This is only because I'll be at a meeting for most of the day. Call me if you have any problems. I expect to be home before you, but remember to take your house key," instructed Sara.

As Tyler rode the bus to school and Jake didn't get on at his usual spot, he assumed his mom drove him that day. When he wasn't in class, Tyler thought about calling him on his cell phone but knew he would get in trouble because he was not to use the phone except to call his mom in an emergency.

Finally, school was over and Tyler was on his way home when he saw the police cars on his block. Walking into his house, someone shouted to him, "Son, may I have a word with you?" Tyler saw it was a policeman and said, "Okay, but first I need to check in with my mom."

"Son, your mom is over at Mrs. Jacobson's house. Please come with me over there," explained the officer. Tyler was feeling scared and guilty. He thought maybe he and Jake were in trouble for going into Mr. Robertson's yard.

Once inside the Jacobson's home, Tyler saw his mom trying to console Mrs. Jacobson. The police officer asked Tyler to sit at the kitchen table and answer some questions. Both of the women looked up as Tyler walked in. Tyler's mom smiled at him the same way when his Granddad died. Now Tyler knew something was very wrong.

"Tyler, when did you last see Jake?" was the first question from the police officer.

"Yesterday after soccer practice," Tyler answered.

"What were you doing?" asked the officer.

"We were, were playing outside," Tyler said tentatively.

The police officer was not satisfied. "Tell me exactly where you were and what you were doing," commanded the officer. Tyler's head was hanging low when he answered, "We kinda played a joke on Mr. Robertson. Jake rang his bell and I was in his backyard trying to see into his basement window."

"Why were you doing this?" inquired the officer. At this point Tyler broke down from fear and guilt and told the three adults everything. All the strange things and the scary way Mr. Robertson looked at them made them want to find out what he was hiding. Then Tyler told them about the old man in the basement lying on a cot.

The officer then pressed on for more details about what happened after they left Mr. Robertson's house. Once Tyler had told them everything, he asked, "What is going on? Where is Jake?" There was silence at this point. Tyler was then told that Jake was missing. He had been seen last by his parents at around 9:00 p.m. when he went to bed.

For some reason, Tyler thought about his little trip outside last night for one last look at old Mr. Robertson's yard. Did Jake do the same thing? Tyler knew that Jake had a secret way to get out of his room. When he slept over, they both used the secret passageway. It was a window in his mother's sewing room that had a trellis outside of it. It would shake as the boys climbed down it.

Tyler told the officer about this secret way to get in and out of the houses. Once all the questions had been answered, Tyler's mother took him home with a promise to Mrs. Jacobson that she would check on her later.

Later that night when Tyler was in bed, Sara wondered if she should have brought up her involvement that day with Mr. Robertson. Taking those pictures and seeing the strange light in the basement seemed unimportant until Tyler told the officer about their prank. Sara decided to call the police. When she told them about the pictures she took, they instructed her to have them available for the police to pick up tomorrow.

With that off her chest, she called her husband and told him everything. He was concerned there was someone loose in the neighborhood, possibly snatching children. They agreed to not send Tyler to school for few days for both his safety and because of his natural concern for Jake.

The next couple days were a blur for Tyler. The police came and went from their home and the neighborhood several times. His mom spent time with the Jacobsons, bringing Tyler with her. Once his dad returned from his trip, the police came back again and Tyler overheard that Mr. Robertson was very ill and was taken to the hospital.

More days passed and still no news about Jake. Then the police came to Tyler's house again and told them that

Mr. Robertson had died. They received a court order to search the house and found lots of laboratory equipment, but nothing that incriminated Mr. Robertson. He had previously explained to the police that he was a chemist and still worked part-time. As for the old man that Tyler had seen, Mr. Robertson denied he existed and the police did not find him.

Tyler was back at school, but only because he had no choice. He could not believe his best friend was gone—missing, with no clue as to where or why. Tyler still believed something was connected to Mr. Robertson, but he had no way to prove it.

When days turned into weeks, it was harder than ever for Tyler to not think about Jake. He couldn't shake the feeling that somehow the prank he and Jake had played on Mr. Robertson had resulted in Jake's disappearance. Tyler blamed himself and grew increasingly depressed.

To help Tyler through this horrible time, his parents decided to get him a dog. He had asked for a dog for years. This seemed like the right time not only because Tyler was old enough, but mostly because he needed a new best friend. After visiting a couple of nearby dog pounds, the family decided to adopt Toby. He was a skinny mixed breed with a shaggy coat of mostly brown with eyes that seemed to reflect intelligence and devotion to the family who cared for him.

Tyler was happy to have his own dog finally, but still thought about Jake everyday. He took Toby for walks to places he and Jake used to go. Toby wanted to go everywhere with Tyler, including school. When Tyler would leave in the morning, Toby would whine and scratch at the door, looking quizzically at Sara as if to ask why he can't go with his boy.

Almost two months had passed since Jake's disappearance. Old Mr. Robertson's house sat dark and silent until today. Sara noticed a moving truck pulled up next door and mentioned it at breakfast that day. Tyler was relieved that someone new was moving in and secretly hoped they had a son his age. Once Tyler was on the bus to school, Sara began to clean up the kitchen. As she took out the trash, Toby sneaked out the door without her noticing.

That morning Sara was very busy on the phone with clients. Hours passed before she noticed Toby was not in the house. After calling him many times, she got worried. Once it was apparent he was not in the house, she frantically looked in the yard. Not seeing him around, she called out for him. Their yard was fenced, but Sara knew that dogs sometimes dug themselves out of a fenced yard. She searched the perimeter of the fence for signs of digging and sure enough she found one. In an effort to trace the direction Toby went she realized he was headed over to the old Robertson property.

Racing over to the house next door, Sara practically barged into her new neighbor. Looking up, she smiled saying, "Hi, I'm Sara, your next door neighbor. I think my dog is in your yard."

"Yes, he is. I'm Roger. Nice to meet you," her new neighbor introduced himself. Sara collected her dog, which growled at the new neighbor.

"Sorry for the trouble. I don't know what's gotten into him. Anyway, welcome to the neighborhood!" responded Sara. "Where are you from?" asked Sara.

"Oh, I move around with my company," was the vague reply from Roger.

"Well, again, welcome and if there's anything we can do for you, just come on over," Sara said moving towards the gate.

As she left she wondered why she felt something was odd about Roger. Sara couldn't put her finger on it, but she didn't get a warm neighborly feeling. When Tyler got home, she told him about their new neighbor with the detail of how Toby made his introduction. That night, they put Toby on a leash in the yard until they could reinforce the fence to prevent his escape.

The following Saturday Tyler and Toby were out on their usual scouts around the neighborhood when they met Roger. As they approached Roger's yard, Toby began to growl. Tyler was surprised because he hadn't heard Toby growl before. With his head bowed telling Toby to settle down, Tyler was met by Roger's commanding voice, "Hello there, young man."

Looking up, Tyler met his new neighbor. "Hi, I'm Tyler.

We live next door," introduced Tyler. Then time stood still. A big toothy grin spread over Roger's face and a large gold tooth popped into view. "I'm Roger. Nice to meet you," replied Roger.

Tyler backed away immediately and said, "I gotta go. Bye." Toby was still growling as Tyler carried him away.

When Tyler got home, he went into the kitchen where his parents were having coffee and laughing about something. Busting into their conversation, Tyler said, "Mom, Dad, that new neighbor is weird. He looks like old Mr. Robertson."

"Son, it's not nice to make statements like that," was his father's response.

"Dad, he has a gold tooth just like old Mr. Robertson!" said Tyler.

"That doesn't mean he looks like him. Gold teeth used to be very popular," explained his dad.

"Well, Toby doesn't like him either," said Tyler. He felt his parents did not understand and went up to his room. Once inside his room, he looked at Toby. Toby was alert and ready for action. Tyler petted Toby and said, "I know and you know that that guy is strange. Let's keep an eye on him."

That night before going to bed, Tyler let Toby out in the yard to do his business. Hooking Toby up to the leash quickly, Tyler went back in to the house to get a snack.

Toby did his usual perimeter of the house security check while doing his business, when the leash quietly clicked off of his collar. Tyler had partially clipped it to the leather part of the collar instead of the metal u-ring and it had loosened itself as Toby moved.

Once loose from the leash, Toby began his work of getting out of their yard and into Roger's yard. Digging a hole to get out didn't take long and Toby scrambled into the next yard. Sniffing around to find what he knew was there, Toby once again began digging.

Tyler finished his bowl of cereal and went out to get Toby. When he saw the leash without Toby on the end of it, Tyler yelled out for him. Going back to the house to turn on lights, Tyler saw the hole that Toby had dug. Following the trail like his mother had done, Tyler was headed into Roger's yard. Seeing Toby working hard at digging a new hole, Tyler ran to his dog.

"What are you doing, boy?" asked Tyler. Toby looked up at him briefly as if to say, watch me and you'll see what I'm doing. The hole was deep now and Toby was still hard at work. Tyler sensed something was there and he and Toby were going to find it. It took longer than Tyler hoped as he stood there in the dark watching shadows cross the windows in Roger's house.

Finally, Toby exaltedly pulled something out of the ground. Tyler didn't know if he was more excited or more scared. Taking it from Toby he ran back to his house with the dog in tow. It was slimy and Tyler had to muster up his courage to even hold it. Once in the street light, he saw what it was. It was a finger from a small hand. Most of the skin was missing.

FOUR

The police determined that the hand belonged to Jake Jacobson, but could not find a connection to Roger in what was now a murder investigation. Roger seemed unconcerned about the police going through his home. When the police questioned him about the unusual equipment he kept in the basement, he explained that he worked for a pharmaceutical company and needed to keep samples on hand.

Tyler's parents discussed moving to a new home. With the final proof that Jake had been murdered and at least a part of his body buried in the yard next door, Tyler's parents did not feel comfortable raising their son in this neighborhood. Tyler was still certain that Roger was part of the crime. Tyler told his parents that he was afraid of Roger, although he was cleared of any connection to the crime. Sara, too, felt that Roger was suspicious. She always felt the hairs rise on her neck when she and Roger crossed paths. And oddly enough, Sara could see a resemblance to

Mr. Robertson too, though she did not mention it.

Allan came home from work a few weeks before Christmas and announced that he had been promoted and they would be moving to North Carolina right after the holidays. They would fly there that weekend to begin house hunting. Sara was only too glad to get away and start a new life.

Christmas came and went with a new house and new neighborhood on the horizon. Thoughts of Jake's unsolved murder still invaded their minds on a daily basis, but they felt the future looked more promising now that their move was only a few days away. Tyler and Toby were on strict orders to stay away from Roger and his yard. Toby still growled every time he saw Roger from across his yard.

On the day of their move, Tyler learned that the new family, the McAndrews, who bought their house, had a son around his age. He also learned that neither his parents nor their realtor told the family about the murder or their suspicions about their next-door neighbor. The family discussed this and they all agreed that without proof, they did not want to spread rumors about Roger. Still, each of them felt uneasy about it.

As the weeks passed and they settled into their new home, memories of the ordeal began to fade. Tyler was making new friends and liked his new school. Both Sara and Allan were happier now that they felt their son was in a safer place and they could put the past behind him. That was until they read the newspaper that Easter morning.

"Ten-year-old boy, Douglas McAndrew, has gone missing from his home in Glen Haven, Arkansas. Ironically, less than one year ago in the exact same neighborhood, an eleven-year-old boy went missing, and later his body parts were found in a nearby backyard. The owner of this home had passed away; however, no evidence linked him to the missing boy. Oddly, the new owner of the same nearby house has also passed away. Police investigated the home again but failed to find any evidence of foul play."

EPILOGUE

Spring came early this year and moving day arrived with the sun shining and the birds singing. Carl, as he called himself, whistled a little tune as he carried boxes into the house. It would take only one more DNA injection to perfect the formula. With any luck he could take care of that later this year. Then, in his new and improved body, he could move away from Glen Haven and start mass producing his formula and making the money that he so deserved.

With his impending fortune on his mind, "Carl" smiled his broad, toothy grin and the one gold tooth sparkled in the sunshine.

No Sign Posted

One

On the northeast side of Chicago in the Rogers Park neighborhood, there was change taking place slowly but surely. Old buildings were boarded up or torn down. Occasionally new ones went up in their places, but mostly the lots stood vacant. The rat population was a growing problem, and signs were posted that rat poison was placed in the areas most frequented.

This neighborhood saw other changes taking place, such as more crime and people leaving for the suburbs. The parks in the neighborhood were run-down and often dangerous because of the drug dealers. Parents told their children to stay away from the parks, so the children would gather in the alleyways and play a game called pinners. Pinners was a game of throwing a ball against a wall and seeing how far it would rebound back. Depending on where the ball went, it would be considered a first, second, or third base hit. Baseball rules were loosely applied and runs scored.

One day the neighborhood kids were playing pinners, and the ball took off around the corner. It skidded into the back entrance of an abandoned grocery store. The children scrambled down the steps leading to the locked back door and looked for their ball. It was fun to climb on the steps and poke their faces into the small window next to the door. The back room where all the boxes of food used to be kept was empty now, but through the door opening, they could see aisles and empty shelves still standing, along with the checkout lanes, minus the cash registers.

Everything that could be sold was gone and the previous owners had sold the building to a real estate developer who took full advantage of the situation. Mr. and Mrs. Oblansky sold their business for far less than market value because they feared the future. Once the big stores took most of their business, they feared debt would overtake them. The couple hoped to retire in a few years and couldn't risk a financial disaster at this time in their lives.

Mr. Lanzini, the real estate developer, played on this fact and made a ridiculously low offer. The storeowners spoke to another real estate developer who pretended to also be interested in buying their property. After hearing the even lower bid that this developer would have made, the Oblanskys took the first offer. Truth was that these two men were friends and liked to help each other get the best deals.

The Oblanskys gathered up their personal belongings and moved to Missouri where they had some family. Life had its ups and downs and the couple felt grateful to still have each other and some savings to keep them afloat.

The neighborhood children liked the couple very much. On hot summer days, ice cream cones sometimes appeared outside the corner store, and many a happy kid enjoyed their generosity. Throughout the years, the Oblanskys participated in community events and always kept a watchful eye out for the children's safety. Since they never had children of their own, they were especially fond of their customers' children and watched them grow with the love and interest of an aunt and uncle.

The children responded with affection and liked to hang around their store. When they heard the news of them selling the business, it was as though a family member was leaving. The children had a special good bye with the Oblansky's, along with many of the parents. The beloved couple provided refreshments on the day before they left. Tears flowed and everyone felt the loss the following day when the small moving truck pulled away with their modest belongings.

It was familiar and somewhat comforting to play by the Oblanskys' old store, so the children picked up their game right there on the steps. One thing led to another and pretty soon the kids were more interested in exploring this little spot in their neighborhood than in playing. As they probed the small window, they discovered it was a fire window, meaning it opened at the top and could be pushed or pulled out. This allowed people to escape in case of a fire.

When the children discovered the window pulled open just enough for them to squeeze through, it was the most exciting moment they had experienced in a long time. One of the older and bigger kids, Jared, said he would go in first and check it out. It wasn't easy to climb through the opening without anything to land on inside, but the thrill of it made anything possible at that point. With his heart pounding and palms sweating, he scrambled inside and fell a few feet to the floor. Looking around he found a large crate to prop against the wall by the window so that the rest of the kids could get in easier.

One by one, all but the most timid of the neighborhood children climbed into the building via their new secret window. This special hideout spot was their favorite place to play. Each time they entered the spooky, empty building they discovered something new to play with or explore. Since there was no electricity in the building, they knew they had to get out of the building before dark. This made it even more exciting.

Soon it became a daily routine to go into the building after school and the children made a pact to not tell anyone outside of their group about it. If their parents found out, all their fun would end and it would be back to playing pinners in the alley.

For weeks, the children the enjoyed this secret adventure after school and on weekends. It was October, and the weather was getting colder and the days shorter. Soon it would be time to set the clocks back one hour. That meant a lot less time to play in the deserted building after school before it became dark.

They knew instinctively their adventure would become a nightmare if they couldn't find their way out of the building because it was too dark.

Two

On a cold and cloudy Saturday in November, Mr. Lanzini brought his son, Anthony, with him to the neighborhood where the Oblansky store was located. Mr. Lanzini had some work to do in the area and would be talking to other retailers. He was interested in buying other buildings, as well.

He brought Anthony to many job sites and learned the best way to handle the inevitable boredom was to let him do a little exploring on his own. Anthony was eleven years old and could be counted on to be back at a designated time.

Mr. Lanzini had a meeting with a general contractor just a few doors down from the old Oblansky store. Since he was planning to buy the other two properties next to the store, he wanted to find out how much money the whole thing would cost him. The general contractor would need at least a couple hours to cost out the project for Mr. Lanzini.

Of course, Mr. Lanzini would not rush in to make offers to the other retailers. He would wait until the storeowners felt the hard pinch of decreased business and became desperate. Then he could swoop in with ridiculously low offers and take both properties. Mr. Lanzini felt pride in his ability to time his business transactions so strategically.

As he reflected silently on how smart he was, Mr. Lanzini's son interrupted his thought and said, "Dad, I'm going to look around for awhile, okay?"

"That's fine, Anthony, I have lots of work to do. Be back here by 5:30 p.m." With that, Anthony was off to explore and see if he could find anything to do.

The neighborhood children were gathering in the alley where they told their parents they would be playing pinners. Instead, they would head over to the Oblansky store after just a couple minutes. They saw Anthony walking toward them. They froze in their tracks and stared at him. No one knew who he was and therefore they could not trust him. Anthony walked up and said, "Hey, anybody want to play some ball?"

The children shrugged and mumbled "no" and "not interested." Anthony was not one to be put off so easily. "Listen, I'm just here while my Dad is working and I'm bored just walking around." He walked closer to them and said with a bold smile, "Well, what are you all doing? Looks like you were going somewhere." The children seemed to soften their stance, sensing that Anthony just wanted to play.

"We're going somewhere. But you can't go," came the retort from Jared.

Anthony said, "I can go anywhere I want to go."

Jared responded by speaking to his group, "Let's go." The children followed Jared. Anthony followed them. Jared turned around and glared at Anthony. "What part of 'bug off' don't you get?" Jared said.

Anthony shrugged his shoulders and said quietly, "I got nothing to do, so I'm going to follow you."

Something about Anthony's honesty got to Jared and he allowed him to follow the group with no further comment. Once they got to the back entrance of the Oblansky store, Jared turned to their new recruit and said in his harshest voice, "You will not tell anyone about this place. Do you understand?"

Anthony was thoroughly intrigued at this point and nodded his head in agreement. Jared opened the window and went through first, as was their usual procedure. One by one the children filed into the abandoned building like soldiers trained to enter enemy camps. Anthony was the last one and didn't need any instruction as he hoisted himself up and climbed in. His heart pounded with excitement.

Once inside, Anthony looked around. While his eyes adjusting to the reduced light, he saw vague shapes, but wasn't sure what he had gotten himself into. Squinting at the children standing near him, he asked, "What is this place?" Jared, always in command, stepped forward and said authoritatively, "It's a store that closed down. Some guy bought it for really cheap and the owners had to move away."

Anthony stiffened when he heard Jared's words. He realized it was his dad who was the "some guy" that they were talking about and he sure didn't want them to know. Acting as nonchalant as possible, he asked, "So, who used to own this place?"

"The Oblanskys. They were real nice. Gave us free ice cream and stuff. They didn't get a fair price for their property, according to my parents. People don't like what happened to them."

Anthony knew his dad liked to brag to his mom about how smart he was and how he made some "big money" when situations turned in his favor. Trying to change the subject, Anthony said, "So what's in this place? Let me look around."

With that, the children showed him some of the neat places to explore. Anthony joined right in and all of the children scattered throughout the empty building, as they did everyday. They were willing to share their secret with Anthony because he didn't live in their neighborhood and couldn't tell on them. Also, he was clearly impressed with how the kids had found this great place. The kids felt his admiration and enjoyed the status it brought.

The children were busy playing and chasing each other for close to two hours when the sun began to set. Being late fall, the sun was setting early. Inside the abandoned building there were no lights to turn on. Once it was dark, it could be very difficult to find the way out of the building.

Jared, always the leader, was the first to notice. He shouted out, "Let's get going. It's getting dark." Everyone within earshot responded by heading to the back window. One by one the children hurriedly took their turn to climb out. Jared looked around after many of the children had climbed out and shouted one more time, "Out everybody now!" At this point, it was completely dark and Jared could not see who was still waiting in line.

This was the darkest it had been when the kids left the building and they were anxious to get out and go home. Once outside the children did not congregate for long. They were worried their parents had been calling them. Not wanting to get in trouble, the children ran in the direction of their homes. It was Naomi who spoke up right before the group departed. "What about Anthony? Where is he?" Jared jumped right in, "He left with us. I think he just went home as soon as he got out."

As Jared ran home, he thought about what he said. He really didn't see Anthony leaving the building, but in the darkness he didn't really see anyone, just shapes and outlines of faces. It was a mass scramble to get everyone out of the building through the small window. With so much noise, Jared felt sure that Anthony couldn't still be in the building. With that final thought, Jared poured on the speed to get home before dinner.

THREE

This was the most fun Anthony had had in a long time. It was scary and a little dangerous, but most of all it was fun to be with other kids. He was happy they let him in on their big secret and, boy, he sure wouldn't tell his dad about it. Dad! Anthony had lost track of time. He was supposed to go back to the car at 5:30 p.m. Anthony looked down at his watch in the increasing darkness, but he couldn't see the time. Pressing the button on the side of his watch, it lighted the face and he could see that it was 5:35 p.m. No wonder it was so dark!

Anthony worried about being late getting back to his dad. His dad was a stickler for being prompt, and Anthony knew he would be in trouble. Crawling out from under an old produce scale where he had been sitting, he looked around but didn't see anyone. It was so dark that he didn't see anything. He had been playing tag with some of the kids and the last person he saw was Nigel. He told him about this great spot to hide and then left to hide some place else.

It was also really quiet now. Anthony strained to hear the other kids and could only hear muffled sounds of traffic outside. He called out and waited for a response. It was a little difficult to remember where he was exactly and how to get to the backroom where the window was. Anthony felt panic rising in his throat and it made him mad at himself. He silently reminded himself that he was eleven years old and not afraid of the dark.

When still no one responded and there were no other sounds inside the building, Anthony then decided the kids had played a joke on him. They were hiding and pretending to not be there so that he would get scared. Anthony was not about to let these kids get the best of him. He would simply walk out of this dumb place and ruin their fun.

Walking was not easy since he couldn't see anything. Determined to not let these kids make a fool out of him, Anthony forced himself to continue walking by holding onto whatever he felt in his path. He forged ahead, or what he thought was ahead, and told himself that eventually he would get to the backroom or begin to make sense of where he was and then know where to go.

It was painstakingly slow and Anthony was not sure if he was dripping with sweat from fear of never getting out of there or of what his dad would do to him when he did. Anthony's dad never hit him, but the fact that his dad would be so disappointed made Anthony feel terrible. He became even more determined to find the room with the window and get out. He would explain to his dad what happened and that he would never do anything like this again.

Feeling his way inch by inch was difficult and taking a very long time. Anthony called out again, "Hey guys, come on. Give me a break here. You've had your fun, now help me get out of here." No answer. Anthony couldn't believe they were still hiding and making him struggle. After several more attempts to get them to talk to him, to end this cruel joke, Anthony broke down.

Tears streamed down his face. He shouted, "Help me! Where is everybody?" With silence answering him every time he pleaded, Anthony realized that no one was hiding and waiting to jump out at him. The sweat pouring down his neck turned into cold fingers trickling down his shirt. He was alone in the dark, abandoned building, and could not find the window to get out.

Crawling, walking, running, Anthony grabbed at the air and struggled to find the way to the window. It was now 7:15 p.m. and for close to two hours, Anthony combed every inch in his path for the way to the backroom. He sobbed hysterically now, and he knew that was not going to help him get out of there. Finally, he fell to his knees and tried to calm down. Since he was struggling so much, he told himself that his dad would somehow know where he was and come get him.

When he finally heard himself yelling out to his dad, he first laughed at himself and then started crying again. It was at that moment that the thought came to him that he should forget the window in the back room and just break a window in the front and climb out that way. Even if he couldn't break the window enough to get out, he could scream and get someone to help him.

Clutching at the counter in front of him, Anthony surmised that he was in the front of the store. There was thick brown paper on all of the windows so no light from the street shone into the building. The brown paper was for security reasons, the Oblanskys were told, and they were required to put it up before they left. Anthony ripped off a large sheet of the brown paper and felt a huge relief as a small stream of light from the street shone into the desolate building.

He was going to get out of here. The light coming from the street told him so. He felt new energy and courage flooding his body.

Now, Anthony looked around for something to throw at the window to break it. There was not a chair or small object anywhere to be found. Anthony was too close to let this discourage him. He went on a rampage looking for anything to use to break the window. Scouring around in the areas where the weak light was shining in, Anthony found a small stack of paper bags, a notebook, some pens and pencils, and finally a broken-down chalkboard that must have been used to advertise specials. It wasn't very sturdy, but Anthony turned it on its side where the metal edge was intact and began to bang it against the glass window.

Again and again, he carefully banged the metal against the window. Keeping his eyes on the lookout, he prayed that if he couldn't break the window, someone would hear him and come to investigate. After a few minutes, the chalkboard collapsed in his hands. Tears overtook Anthony once again, and he collapsed on the floor.

Getting to his feet, Anthony told himself there was something in this place that would break the window and he was going to find it. With somewhat renewed strength, Anthony looked everywhere again. Going behind a small raised desk area and feeling his way inch by inch, his hands felt a small flower vase with tiny roses etched on it.

Anthony clutched the small vase in his hands as though it was a torch. Running to the window where the paper was torn off, Anthony banged the vase against the glass. He knew he couldn't hit it too hard and risk breaking the vase. Maybe his best chance was to bang it repeatedly and wait for someone to hear him. Eventually, someone had to hear him.

Carefully and methodically, Anthony banged the vase against the window. He tried to vary the beat so that people would not get accustomed to the noise and ignore it. Hours passed and Anthony kept hitting the window. He looked at his watch and it was 2:19 a.m. Though he had been through the worst ordeal of his short life, Anthony knew that once the sun came up, he would get out of here.

FOUR

The wrecking crew arrived early at the job site. They were professionals who took their work and the safety seriously. John Elburn, the supervisor, was the first to arrive, as usual. He walked around the Oblansky store several times to be sure nothing was present that would prevent the crew from taking the building down.

As he passed the front of the store, he noticed a sheet of the brown paper had been torn down from the inside. He immediately went to look closer at it for any type of problem. Sometimes vandals did this type of thing, but they never stayed around.

Peering inside the store as best he could, John didn't see anything unusual. Pausing to make a note on his report about the torn sheet John thought he heard something. Straining his ears, John stood there for another minute. Hearing nothing more, he moved on. Had to be a rat, he mused. They inhabit more buildings in Chicago than people ever knew. These rats were about to have their happy home destroyed.

John walked to the front door of the old store to tear off the notice stating that the building would be demolished today and all the legal mumbo-jumbo. It was a necessary document for his report. Not seeing it attached to the front door, John grumbled this one might have blown off. However, the notice was required to be posted on all doors, so John walked around to the back.

At the back door, the crew had assembled and was awaiting John's instructions. "Is the notice on the door?" asked John of his men. Looking first at the door and then around it, the men confirmed John's suspicions. There was no notice posted on this building.

Muttering a few choice words, John grabbed his cell phone and called Lanzini's office. Lanzini was known to break the rules and John did not like working with him. After speaking to his secretary, Ellen, John found out that Lanzini had a family emergency. John stated simply that he would reschedule the demolition after the notice had been posted.

Ellen was urgently begging him not to do this. "He will have a fit if this building is not gone today," she said nervously. John explained that the notice was legally required to be posted for seventy-two hours prior to the demolition even though he knew she was well aware of this. "Please, John, I will backdate the notice. Please take care of it today. Mr. Lanzini will fire me even though he is the one who is supposed to put up the notice."

John hung up saying he'll do it, but this will be the last time he bends the rules for this guy. Ordering his crew to begin the work, John disgustedly filled in the information on his report. As he did this, he told his foreman to do the walk-thru. This was the final check to be sure no one was still in the building. Greg, his foreman, was in his late twenties and worked hard to succeed in his profession.

Greg was at the back door and after unlocking it, walked into the building and called out several times. This was not a challenging part of the job. It was rare to find anyone in a building slotted for demolition. Standing in the middle of the store, Greg continued to call out stating the building was about to be torn down and they needed to know if anyone was still inside. It was almost 7:00 a.m. and they needed to begin the preparation work to demolish the building.

Anthony lay crumbled on the floor fast asleep. He had banged the vase against the glass window until 4:30 a.m. to no avail. Eventually, his strength gave out and he closed his eyes while leaning against the wall. During the night Anthony was sure that someone, perhaps a police officer, would hear him and come into the building. When hour after hour passed and no one came, Anthony sadly concluded that he would be in the biggest trouble of his life when he got out of the building in the morning and called his parents.

It had been hard to stay awake until the wee hours of the morning and now Anthony was in a very deep sleep. He slept so soundly that he did not hear Greg yelling just a few yards from him. Nor did he hear the crew working right outside the building. Anthony slept peacefully as the men prepared to demolish the old building.

The crew worked quickly and efficiently to prepare the building site for the wreaking ball. Glass would come shattering out of the building, so the area had to be secured. Once ready, the supervisor would give the go ahead for the huge wrecking ball to do its work.

John never rushed the work, but he also didn't take unnecessary time getting down to business. His crew was known to be the best in the industry and John took pride in his men. Everything was ready now and John gave the go ahead signal as he continuously surveyed the job site.

The noise was intense and that is why the crew all wore earplugs. The surrounding neighborhood would be punished with this noise for only an hour or so as a building this size would come down rather quickly. It was after 9:00 a.m. when the first strike of the ball hit the building.

Dreams flooded Anthony's head as he lay sleeping. It had been the worst night of his young life and he was processing it through his mind in a most bizarre and surreal way. First he was running through a tunnel and screaming for help. Then he was in an ocean with waves crashing upon him and the noise was unbearable. He felt certain his eardrums were pierced from the overwhelming noise.

Struggling to get away from these waves and the

surrounding noise, Anthony thrashed about in his sleep. Finally, his mind allowed him to wake up, but he could not tell that he was awake. The noise was even louder now that he was no longer asleep. The ground seemed to be moving. Looking up, he saw the glass windows in front of him crashing in.

With the vase still clutched in his hand, Anthony ran to the back room to climb out of the building. He reached the window and shoved it out with all his might. With the window open for him to crawl out, he turned around and saw a cyclone of whirling debris chasing him.

Five

Years passed, and the neighborhood kids had long since grown up and moved away.

Jared became a math teacher and lived in a nearby suburb. His wife, Natalie, also a teacher, was expecting their first child. Today they were visiting Jared's mom, who still lived in the old neighborhood. In fact, she still lived in the same apartment building where Jared and his sister grew up. It was about a block away from the old Oblansky grocery store.

The Oblansky grocery store was now a twenty-four-hour convenience store. It had been torn down, and then strangely, the lot sat vacant for years. It became another one of those empty lots filled with garbage and who knows what. Eventually, the land was sold once again and the new developer built this store.

Jared and Natalie wanted Josie, Jared's mom, to come to their house for Thanksgiving dinner. Josie would have none of that and insisted she cook the whole meal for them at her apartment. When Jared and Natalie arrived,

Josie was humming away in the kitchen. They kissed and hugged her and smelled the delicious aromas of a feast in the making. Realizing that she needed an extra onion and perhaps more bread, she asked her son to run down to the store. It sounded like old times. Only this time, it was an impersonal larger store with very high prices.

Jared was happy to help out and quickly got his coat to leave. It was chilly outside and the sky was dark even though it was only 4 p.m. Only a block away, Jared sprinted to the store and nearly knocked over an older man who seemed to jump out of nowhere. "I'm sorry. I didn't see you," explained Jared. Barely looking up, the scruffy man mumbled something, but Jared didn't understand him.

Jared bought the items and left the store. He was looking out for this man to be sure he didn't bump into him again. It worried Jared that this man seemed homeless and could be a danger to his mother.

Back inside the apartment, the women talked excitedly about the layette that Josie was knitting for the baby. The yarn was yellow because they didn't know if the baby was a boy or girl. Seeing his brother-in-law, Alec, looking a bit lost in the shuffle, Jared asked him if he wanted to play a game of pinners.

"What the heck is pinners?" asked Alec who had been raised in the country. "It's like baseball only on a smaller scale," answered Jared. "I'm in," replied Alec who was already feeling claustrophobic in the small apartment.

The men went out the back door and down the steps to the alley where Jared had actually played this same game during his childhood. After Jared explained the basics of the game to Alec, they began playing. After a couple minutes, Alec had gotten the hang of it and they were enjoying a lively game.

With sweat pouring down their faces, even though it was one of the colder Thanksgivings on record, they stopped to catch their breath. Turning they saw a couple of boys walking toward them. "Hey, are you guys playing pinners?" asked the taller boy.

"Yep, do you want in on the game?" replied Jared.

"I think I know how to play. But it's an old-timers' game. Nobody plays it anymore," stated the boy.

"Well, let's just see if the old-timers can beat the newbies" jested Alec, who was now heavily into the game.

The four of them played pinners for almost an hour. It was 15-9, old-timers, when they called it quits. Laughing and out of breath, Jared told the boys that he grew up in this neighborhood and played this game nearly every day. The boys jokingly said they let them win for old time's sake. It was a good-natured bit of fun, but it was time to get back inside with the family.

Because Jared didn't want to alarm his mother, he asked the two boys about the homeless man at the convenience store. "Oh, you mean old Lanzini," replied the Zachary, the shorter boy. "He hangs around the store everyday holding onto a little piece of glass or something, He's crazy, but he doesn't bother anyone."

At this point, Jacob, the taller one, came forward and said, "Old Lanzini says he hears his son calling out to him from inside the store. That's why he hangs around."

"What do you mean?" asked Jared.

"His son disappeared a long time ago. Lanzini used to be a big hot shot and bought buildings and stuff. His son disappeared one day. It was right at the time they tore down the old store where the White Hen is now," explained Jacob.

Jared's pulse rate shot up and he felt his temples throbbing. He felt dizzy as he tried to recall the exact events of a day long ago in November when a new kid joined them in the abandoned Oblansky store. "What was his son's name?" asked Jared looking at the boys.

The boys shrugged and then Jacob said, "Maybe it was Anthony. He calls it out once in while."

The blood drained from Jared's face. He wouldn't have been able to recall the name on his own, but hearing it confirmed in his mind who the boy was. "Let's get going, Alec," Jared said in a hoarse voice.

Thanksgiving dinner was not the celebration it should have been for Jared. His mind kept going back to that day when a new kid went into the old abandoned store with them. It had gotten dark and they all climbed out and went home before they could have known that Anthony had not come with them.

As the family said their good-byes and Jared kissed his mom's cheek, he told himself this was all a strange coincidence. Anthony got out of the building, along with the other kids and something terrible had happened to him afterward. That was his final thought as he pulled away from his mom's apartment.

Almost without realizing it, Jared turned left instead of right and drove by the convenience store. Natalie asked sleepily, "Why are you going the long way, Babe?"

"I want to get a pack of gum to help me stay awake," replied Jared.

Looking out for Mr. Lanzini, Jared walked into the store and bought his gum. Leaving the store, he walked around to the back and saw a slumped over figure in the alley. "Mr. Lanzini, is that you?" asked Jared.

"Did you see my boy? Anthony! Have you seen him?" asked Mr. Lanzini in a slurred voice.

"No, sir, I haven't seen him. I'm sorry," answered Jared. Not wanting to upset him, Jared turned to leave. Mr. Lanzini looked back down at the little broken vase in his hand. The tiny roses on it were almost worn away from his hands holding it.

All in Due Time

One

It was Melissa Cloverdale's first day of school as a fourth-grade teacher. She graduated last spring with honors and was eager to begin her career. Melissa awoke before her alarm went off and practically jumped out of bed. She went about her morning routine carefully enough to look her best on this special day, but at a much faster pace because she was so excited to finally be in her own classroom teaching!

When Melissa arrived at school she was among the first few teachers to show up. They were also new and eager to begin. Walking into the building, she smiled warmly at Miss Andrews, whom she had seen at the new teacher orientation. It was school policy to use only proper names, so Melissa did not know her first name. They were both anxious to appear professional and calm, as teachers were supposed to be. Nonetheless, Miss Andrews likewise flashed an eager smile at Melissa.

After checking in at the school office and obtaining her badge, she walked confidently to her classroom, number

201. She felt exhilaration as she pushed open the door and entered what was to become her domain. The room felt stuffy and strangely different than it had a few weeks prior, when she met with the principal, Mr. Danver, and the assistant principal, Miss Archer. The three of them had spoken for well over an hour in this room. During that meeting, Melissa had felt at ease in the room and was surprised at how oddly familiar the room had felt to her. The meeting had been pleasant, although Melissa was surprised at how few actual questions they had asked her. She wasn't sure how well she did in the interview because both the principal and assistant principal were difficult to read. They maintained a rather still, formal demeanor and never reacted positively or negatively to anything she said.

Miss Archer, a thin, well-dressed woman, probably in her late forties, had eyebrows that were dramatically penciled in giving her an expression of chronic surprise. She spoke in a hushed tone as though everything she said was highly confidential. Mr. Danver, with his nearly bald head, stately posture, and portly girth had a calm and patronizing demeanor. They had seemed concerned about her ability to blend in with the school's culture. When Melissa asked them to explain, they were unnaturally reticent about giving her specifics beyond the utmost important requirement of adhering to school policy in all matters.

Their meeting took place after she had attended an afternoon tea. There she met teachers who had been at this school for years. They greeted Melissa with polite smiles, but Melissa couldn't shake the feeling they were "tolerating" her. Melissa asked them if they had any advice for her but their responses were pretty much all the same. In one version or another, they crooned, "Teach the lessons from the textbooks and everything will work out fine." Any gestures of friendship on Melissa's part were met with cool non-committal responses.

Later, when speaking with Mr. Danver and Miss Archer about adhering to school policy, Melissa surmised that rule included no real conversations between teachers and probably no friendships with them as well. This was something that puzzled Melissa, but in her excitement, she put that in the back of her mind and focused on anticipating the needs of her class.

As soon as Melissa entered her classroom, she opened the windows and felt the slightest breeze. It was still summer and the air was heavy. She decided that tomorrow she would bring in a fan to get the air circulating. She would also ask the office if the air conditioning was working properly. She went about the business of unloading her briefcase, a graduation gift from her parents, and setting up her desk. She could have sworn that the desk was larger and much nicer during her interview. Oh well, she was not concerned about that and the students would begin arriving in less than ten minutes. She had her lessons prepared for the first month, but she knew adjustments would be made as real life unfolded. With a warm smile on her face, Melissa sat poised for the influx of her students. One by one, rather reluctantly, children began to file in and take seats. She offered a cheerful, "Good Morning!" but it was returned with only half nods and grunts. Once it appeared that everyone was seated, Melissa formally introduced herself by writing her name on the board. Facing the class with a beaming smile, she proceeded to tell them how very pleased she was to start the new school year with them.

The children sat expressionless and waited for her next move. Melissa had secretly hoped for some enthusiasm from her class, but her training had taught her to not let unmet expectations alter her demeanor. Carrying on with her plan to provide some brief details about herself and then diving right into the lesson plan, Melissa projected a teacher with a passionate interest in her work. By lunchtime, the children showed some enthusiasm. While the children were at lunch, Melissa got herself a glass of water, pulled out her small lunch bag, and reviewed the rest of the day's lesson. She was pleased that her students had perked up and wanted to continue that momentum. At that moment, Melissa felt certain that all of her years of education and training were worth every minute, and teaching was what she was meant to do.

Once the children were seated again, Melissa smiled and welcomed them back. The children looked strangely suspicious at this. Melissa then launched into their next lesson with the same enthusiasm as earlier. Once again, the children began showing interest and their new teacher made extra efforts to spark their desire to learn. Suddenly, the classroom door opened and Mr. Danver entered. Melissa was caught off guard. Mr. Danver asked if he might speak with her in the hall. "Of course, I'll be right there," she responded. Melissa instructed her class to continue reading the chapter silently and told them she would return momentarily.

In the hall, Mr. Danver looked at her with a rather stern expression and said he would need to speak with her in his office. Another teacher would fill in for her. Melissa wondered if she had done something wrong. Why else would she be removed from her classroom in the middle of a lesson?

Mr. Danver led her to what she thought would be his office, but instead he took a turn and led her downstairs. She did not want to appear anxious, but when she caught up with him, she asked him where they were going. He responded with a curt, "Just follow me, Miss Cloverdale." Melissa obeyed and continued to follow him, but her heart pounded. He led her into a small room and instructed her to be seated. There was a table and one chair in the room and nothing else. Melissa sat down and immediately asked Mr. Danver to explain what this was all about. Mr. Danver responded with the slightest smile and said, "All in due time." He then left the room and closed the door. Melissa felt actual panic rise in her throat as she called out, "Mr. Danver, come back and tell me what is going on!" When Mr. Danver did not respond to her plea, Melissa exclaimed, "What in the world is going on?" After a minute or two, Melissa decided she would simply not tolerate being treated like this. She would leave the room, find Mr. Danver, and get to the bottom of this. She turned the doorknob forcefully. It did not turn. The door was locked. She shook the knob and then pounded on the door. This was ridiculous. Why was she in a locked room?

Two

Melissa sat down to compose herself. There must be a reasonable explanation. She ran through the possibilities for this and concluded that she must have failed to provide some vital document and the school could not allow her to teach until they had it. The safety and concern for the children must come first and schools had to be sure their teachers were above reproach. With this thought in mind, Melissa once again went to the door and this time, knocked on it and called out, "Mr. Danver, please speak to me. I'm sure I can correct any oversight on my part."

When more than fifteen minutes passed without a response, Melissa again pounded on the door and demanded someone release her. She heard a slight clicking sound coming from down the hall and pressed her ear to the door. Someone was coming to rescue her! Relief flooded her body as the door was unlocked and clicked open. To her surprise, in walked Miss Archer. In her agitated state of mind, Melissa reached out for Miss Archer's hand and exclaimed, "Thank you, Miss Archer. I don't know what's happened, but I'm certain it can all be worked out." Miss Archer gave her the slightest smile and then in her usual whispering tone said, "All in due time, dear. All in due time." Miss Archer handed Melissa a small glass of water and instructed her to drink it and then promptly left. The door was once again closed without any chance for Melissa to protest.

Putting the glass down on the table, Melissa stared at the door dumbfounded. She felt weak in the knees and had to sit down. Why was this happening? What were her students thinking? She was gone for more than thirty minutes. Who was filling in for her? In Melissa's experience, people did not do strange things; therefore, there had to be a reasonable explanation for Mr. Danver to lock her in a room and then send Miss Archer in a with a glass of water. With fear climbing up her spine, Melissa concluded that something dreadful had happened to her family and they were trying to prepare her for the shock. With shaking hands, she reached for the glass of water and gulped it down in an effort to bolster her strength.

Oddly enough, drinking the water did calm her down. She felt almost too calm. In her mind, she realized this was a strange reaction, but she quickly rationalized it by thinking that she must be in shock. Shock feels like calm, only you aren't able to function. Slowly, she saw that she could not move her body when she wanted to. She wanted to get up from the table and knock on the door again . . . except she couldn't move. Her head felt heavy and laying it on the table seemed like the best thing to do. Her eyes were twitching and soon she had to close them.

What she didn't know is that she actually slid off the chair onto the floor and lay there for several hours.

THREE

Her head felt like rocks had been stuffed inside it as she tried to pull herself up from the floor. The room began to sway as Melissa forced her eyes to focus. Looking around, the table and chair were the only furnishings, but out of the corner of her eye, she saw a paper clip on the floor. With her head pounding, she quickly grabbed it and scanned the room once again for any possible way to escape. Melissa knew she was in trouble.

The door was locked but Melissa knew that people could pick locks, at least in the movies. With nothing to lose, she straightened the paper clip halfway and maneuvered it in the lock. It was a lot easier in the movies. She continued to struggle, causing the door to rattle. The door was a thin, poorly constructed type and the lock was no better. For once Melissa was thankful for the school's low budget when she could feel the doorknob beginning to move. Her efforts to pick the lock were only marginally helpful, but combined with shaking the door and jiggling the doorknob, Melissa was finally rewarded when the door clicked open.

Fighting the temptation to dash right out, Melissa peered out the door in both directions. Her pulse pounded as she saw it was dark in the corridor and almost impossible to see the staircase leading to the main floor. She could not remember which way she came from when Mr. Danver led her to this room. She realized she was in the basement of the building. This frightened her even more. Without knowing which way to go, she decided to go left because she thought she remembered turning right into the room. As she ventured out into the corridor, dark shadows loomed around her. She prayed they were mops and brooms. It was slow going because she couldn't see but it felt better than staying in that room another minute. She was half-running with her hands out in front of her when she fell. Stumbling to get up, she reached out and groped for the wall when she felt what she had been hoping for – the staircase. She raced up the steps and saw there was moonlight streaming into the otherwise dark building. Just thinking about getting to the door and pushing it open relieved her.

Four

She was still on the lookout for anyone, especially Mr. Danver and Miss Archer. The first floor appeared to be empty, so Melissa headed straight for the main entrance. Just as she was about to push open the door, she saw the small alarm box to the right of it. If she opened the door, the alarm would go off. That should bring the police, which would be a welcome relief, but what if Mr. Danver got there first? After this ordeal, Melissa could not take the chance. She headed for the office where she would call the police first and then open the door. Feeling like freedom and safety were within her grasp, Melissa didn't notice the small brown briefcase on the desk. She pushed through the swinging half-door, meant to keep students from freely entering and practically bumped into Miss Andrews. Melissa nearly jumped out of her skin at first, but when she saw it was Miss Andrews, she felt relieved.

"H-hello. Miss Andrews, can you h-help me?" Melissa asked breathlessly. "I've been trapped in a room in the basement for hours. Mr. Danver brought me there. I need to speak with the police," explained Melissa. Miss Andrews looked calmly at her and said, "Of course, dear. Come this way." Melissa thought it was odd how calm and in charge Miss Andrews sounded, but she felt so glad to see a friendly face, she shrugged it off.

When Miss Andrews led her out of the office, Melissa stopped her. "I need to use the phone now!" exclaimed Melissa. Miss Andrews gave her a mock stern expression and said, "Now you know the phone system does not work after school hours." Melissa was not going to trust this brand new teacher without checking it herself. Melissa grabbed the phone and punched one of the buttons to obtain an outside line. Nothing happened. She tried dialing nine first to get an outside line. Again, nothing. After a few more feeble attempts, Melissa apologized, saying, "I'm sorry Miss Andrews. I'm very upset. Let's just get out of here."

When they reached the main door, Miss Andrews held it open for Melissa. When the alarm did not go off, Melissa asked why. Miss Andrews smiled sweetly at her but did not answer.

They walked down the steps and Melissa turned to go to the parking lot while Miss Andrews continued straight ahead. Melissa shouted at her now, "I need to get to the police. I don't have my car keys so we'll need to take your car." Miss Andrews still had that sweet smile on her face when she replied, "No dear, I have a better idea. Let's go to the nearest home and ask them to make the call." Melissa felt a strange sensation in the pit of her stomach in response to Miss Andrew's idea but again she dismissed it.

In her present state, she had no energy to resist, so Melissa turned and walked with Miss Andrews.

The neighborhood around the school was filled with quaint little homes that had immaculate tiny yards around them. Summer flowers were still blooming in their clay pots on well-lit porches. It gave Melissa a sense of security to see the orderly row of houses. She believed her troubles were over.

Miss Andrews directed her to one of the larger homes and said, "We'll get help here, dear." Melissa was glad to finally be somewhere safe where help would be on its way. Up the cobblestone walkway to the front door the two young women walked. The fragrant flowers on the freshly painted white porch filled Melissa's nostrils and calmed her nerves as they waited for someone to answer. A very small woman well into her eighties appeared at the door. She was dressed neat as a pin and her eyes were equally sharp. "Well, hello, what may I do for you?" the woman asked in a quick, clear voice.

Melissa stepped forward and said, "Ma'am, I need to speak with the police. May I use your phone?"

Without another word, the older woman ushered both Melissa and Miss Andrews into her home. Melissa waited for her to say something about calling the police, but instead, their hostess said, "Please sit down, dears, you look dreadfully tired." Her living room looked like a tiny showcase in a museum. Though sparsely furnished, everything was perfectly placed and spotless. Melissa didn't know where to sit because it looked like no one had ever actually sat in this room. Miss Andrews patted the spot next to her on the small sofa and Melissa quickly sat down.

Melissa looked up expectantly in the direction of the tiny woman, but she had vanished. Looking at Miss Andrews, Melissa said, "Oh good, she must be calling the police, or bringing the phone to me so I can call them." A few minutes passed, and the woman appeared in the doorway with a silver tray on which sat all the makings of an afternoon tea. Melissa was surprised but felt reassured by this unexpected hospitality. Obviously, their kind hostess had called the police, and was now helping the girls pull themselves together while they waited.

Miss Andrews didn't hesitate to help herself to tea and a couple of tiny sugar cookies. Melissa gratefully accepted the tea poured by the kindly old woman. As Melissa held the fragile porcelain cup and saucer in her hands, she breathed a sigh of relief. It would all be over soon enough, and Melissa could go home and crawl into bed. She didn't want to think about tomorrow at this point. It would take all of her strength to explain this crazy ordeal to the police. As she sank deeper into the little sofa with the tea warming her up, she caught herself dozing off. Shaking her head to snap back to attention, Melissa noticed her vision was blurry. She murmured, "I'm suddenly very tired. Please excuse my yawning." Both Miss Andrews and the old woman smiled sweetly at her. "I think I'll go wait on the porch for the police. The night air will do me good," Melissa said dreamily.

Melissa struggled to get up from the sofa, and at that precise moment, three more people filed into the tiny room. Melissa looked up at them quizzically. She was still trying to get her eyes to focus when she saw that Mr. Danver and Miss Archer were two of the three people. A low gasp escaped from her throat as she lunged towards the door, practically on her hands and feet. She struggled to get away from them but her body was not cooperating, and her voice was a muffled sob. As she looked up, she saw five people hovering over her and in her terror, she could hear them talking but was not able to make out one single word. It was like a tape running that was sped up making the words incomprehensible.

Melissa felt like she was drowning as the five people swarmed over her. In her weak efforts to break away from them, she had been holding her breath. Now she gasped for air and as quickly as she did, all five of her captors began blowing on her. The air coming out of their mouths was like steam that had a power source all its own. Melissa had no choice but to breathe in the steam. Within seconds, her struggling ceased, her limbs went slack and Melissa rolled to the floor.

FIVE

The feeling of fall was in the air and the sun was less potent now. Leaves started to turn brilliant shades of red, orange, and yellow. The sky had a smoky hue, and as evening fell, one felt inclined to seek the comforts of home and hearth. A group of fourth grade girls were walking home from the library when the subject turned to their teacher, Miss Cloverdale. Ariel, who was the most outspoken of this group, said, "I really thought Miss Cloverdale was different. That first day of school she was so interesting, at least until she left when Mr. Danver came to get her. It must have been a family tragedy. She's not been the same since." Brianna, whose plans and dreams included everything but school, expressed it by saying, "Who cares? They're all the same. School is so boring. I'm going to be an actress!" Elle was the shy one in the group but still felt compelled to chime in, "Miss Cloverdale didn't even remember telling us that we could write our own script for the holiday play this year. When Nathan reminded her, she told him he must be mistaken. I know she said we could."

The conversation drifted on and the girls parted for their homes. The homework was done with minimal effort. As long as they showed up for class and turned in the assignments, no questions were asked. Grades were basically C's whether effort was put into them or not. The children had quickly figured this out and knew that nothing would change.

Epilogue

The morning sky was a brilliant blue with streaks of white clouds. A crisp feeling in the air prompted Melissa to take her jacket. "Better to be safe than sorry," she said cautiously to herself. She arrived at school just before the bell went off and gave a curt nod to the other teachers as she entered the school building. Arriving at her classroom, Melissa pulled out her attendance sheet. The students filed in without greeting and Miss Cloverdale announced they would state the Pledge of Allegiance. In a group voice devoid of feeling, they dutifully said the morning pledge. Next came attendance with low murmurs of acknowledgement. A hand flew up from the back of the classroom.

"Yes, Elle, what is it?" asked Miss Cloverdale sharply. "Teacher, when will we start working on the holiday play?" In a bold move, unlike her, Elle added, "You said we could write our own script. You said it on the first day of school!"

Miss Cloverdale came from behind her desk and folded her arms across her chest as she stared at Elle. "My name is not teacher. It is Miss Cloverdale. Are we quite clear on that?" came the rebuff. "As to the matter of writing our own script that is ridiculous. There is a perfectly good script that the fourth grade classes have been using for the past forty-nine years. There is no need to reinvent the wheel," stated Miss Cloverdale in a clipped tone.

Elle had shrunk back into her chair and did not entertain a response. Nathan however, spoke up, "Miss Cloverdale," he said, exaggerating the syllables of her proper name, "Exactly when is it that we will begin practicing this forty-nine-year-old play?" His belligerence was not lost on the class or on Miss Cloverdale.

"All in due time, children. All in due time," was the thin-lipped reply.

Lightning Source UK Ltd.
Milton Keynes UK
08 September 2010

159620UK00001B/407/P

9 781609 111113